# YOUNG SANTA

# Dan Greenburg

# YOUNG SANTA

ILLUSTRATED BY

Warren Miller

VIKING

VIKING
Published by the Penguin Group
Viking Penguin, a division of Penguin Books USA Inc.,
375 Hudson Street, New York, New York 10014, U.S.A.
Penguin Books Ltd, 27 Wrights Lane, London W8 5TZ, England
Penguin Books Australia Ltd, Ringwood, Victoria, Australia
Penguin Books Canada Ltd, 2801 John Street, Markham, Ontario, Canada L3R 1B4
Penguin Books (N.Z.) Ltd, 182–190 Wairau Road, Auckland 10, New Zealand

Penguin Books Ltd, Registered Offices: Harmondsworth, Middlesex, England

First published in 1991 by Viking Penguin, a division of Penguin Books USA Inc.
Published simultaneously in Canada

1  3  5  7  9  10  8  6  4  2

Text copyright © Dan Greenburg, 1991
Illustrations copyright © Warren Miller, 1991
All rights reserved
Library of Congress Catalog Card Number: 91-50260
I S B N  0 - 6 7 0 - 8 3 9 0 5 - 1
Printed in U.S.A.    Set in 12 point Plantin

FOR YOUNG ZACK

WHEN SOPHIE AND MILTON Claus had their baby, at first they couldn't think what to name him.

"Why don't we name him Otto, after my father?" said Sophie Claus.

"Otto Claus," said Milton. "Hmmm. No, I don't really care for the ring of that, somehow."

"Well, then," said Sophie, "there's my brother Seymour. Why don't we name him Seymour?"

"Seymour Claus, Seymour Claus," said Milton. "I don't know, Sophie. Seymour isn't bad, but I don't really think that's it, either."

"Okay, then," said Sophie, "there's my sister's accountant, Morty."

"Morty Claus, Morty Claus," said Milton. "No, Sophie, we just don't have it yet."

They thought of many names, there in the hospital in Sioux City, Iowa. They thought of Sheldon, Keith, Sheppy, Byron, Marvin, Freddy, and Cornelius. They thought of Julius, Nat, Ralph, Orson, Arnold, Nelson, and Mel. Nothing really clicked for them.

"If you don't come up with a name soon," said a disapproving hospital nurse, "we shall have to simply put 'Baby Claus' on the birth certificate. Do you want us to do *that?*"

Sophie and Milton were upset. They certainly did not want the hospital to simply put "Baby Claus" on the birth certificate. They knew they had to think up a name, and they knew they had to think it up fast.

"You know," said Sophie, smiling, "we had such a lovely vacation last month in Santa Fe. Why don't we name the baby *Santa?*"

"Santa?" said Milton. "Santa . . . Claus?"

"Don't say no until you've rolled it around on your tongue for a while," said Sophie.

"Santa Claus. *Santa* Claus. Santa *Claus,*" said Milton, rolling it around on his tongue. "Hmmm."

"It kind of grows on you, doesn't it?" asked Sophie, watching Milton's face expectantly.

"You know," said Milton, "if anybody had told me last week I'd be sitting in a hospital tonight, thinking about naming my kid after some city in New Mexico, I'd have said they were nuts. But I got to be honest with you. It certainly is different. It certainly is . . . distinctive."

"Then you like it?" said Sophie, delighted.

Milton shrugged and smiled.

"I guess I like it," he said.

"Then Santa it is," said Sophie Claus.

The nurse sighed and wrote down *Santa Claus* on the birth certificate.

T W O

SANTA'S FATHER, MILTON, sold small iceboxes door to door from the back of a station wagon for the Kool Kupboard Kompany in Sioux City, Iowa. The Clauses were not wealthy, but they were comfortable.

One day when little Santa was three years old, Milton's boss called him into his office.

"Milton," said his boss, "my sister's husband needs a job, so I'm giving him your territory here in Sioux City."

"You can't do that," said Milton Claus. "Can you?"

"Of course I can do that," said his boss. "I can do anything I want, because I'm the boss. Fortunately for you, Milton, an opening has just come up in another territory. So we're transferring you and your family to the new territory a week from Thursday. I think you'll be pleased."

"Uh, where's the new territory?" said Milton, nervously. He liked Sioux City and didn't particularly want to be transferred, unless of course the new territory was someplace nice, like Florida or maybe Santa Fe.

"We're transferring you to the North Pole," said Milton's boss.

"The North *Pole,*" said Milton. "You're kidding me."

"No, I'm quite serious, I assure you," said Milton's boss.

"Who's going to want to buy small iceboxes at the North *Pole?*" said Milton. "You might as well send me to *Siberia,* for crying out loud."

Milton's boss glanced briefly at a sales territory map on his wall. It had pins with little red flags on the ends to mark the locations of Kool Kupboard Kompany salesmen all over the world.

"We *do* happen to have an opening coming up in Siberia, as a matter of fact," said Milton's boss. "If you think you'd prefer that."

"No, no, no," said Milton quickly, "the North Pole will be okay, I guess. Unless . . ."

"Unless what?" said his boss.

"Unless," said Milton, "you have something in, say, Florida or Santa Fe?"

Milton's boss looked at the sales map on the wall again.

"Nope," he said. "Nothing in Florida and nothing in

Santa Fe. The North Pole or Siberia would be the only two openings I got at the present time. Take your pick."

"Okay, then," sighed Milton. "I guess I'll take the North Pole."

"I think you'll enjoy the change," said his boss, smiling pleasantly.

T H R E E

MILTON WENT HOME TO tell Sophie and little Santa the news.

"You'll never guess where they're transferring me," said Milton glumly.

"Where, Dada?" said little Santa.

"Guess," said Milton.

"The North Pole," said Sophie.

"Uh, yeah," said Milton. "How did you know?"

"You just had a North Pole kind of expression on your face," she said. "But why do you look so glum?"

"Why do I look so glum?" said Milton. "Get serious. Who's going to want to buy iceboxes at the North *Pole?*"

"Milton, dear, people need iceboxes wherever they are," said Sophie.

She rather liked Sioux City and was disappointed to

hear they would be leaving, but she had always believed in looking on the bright side.

"Dada, is the North Pole like Sioux City?" asked little Santa.

"Not exactly," said Sophie.

"What's different about it?" asked little Santa.

"Well," said Sophie, "at the North Pole, they have a lot less people than in Sioux City and a lot more glaciers."

"That's putting it mildly," said Milton.

"What are glaciers?" asked little Santa.

"Glaciers?" said Sophie. "Glaciers are very long, very wide, very thick sheets of ice. They cover the ground in countries where it snows more than it melts."

"Could I go sledding on glaciers?" asked little Santa.

"You could," said Milton.

"And could I go ice skating on glaciers?" asked little Santa.

"You could," said Milton.

"And could I go skiing on glaciers?" asked little Santa.

"You could," said Milton.

"And could I go tobogganing on glaciers?" asked little Santa.

"You bet your sweet life you could," said Milton.

"Then let's go to the North Pole, Dada," said little Santa happily.

"One problem," said Milton, "is, station wagons don't get much traction on glaciers. What am I supposed to haul my iceboxes around in, a sleigh?"

"I'm sure a sleigh would do just fine," said Sophie.

"Yeah?" said Milton. "And what would I get to pull the sleigh? They don't have Clydesdale horses at the North Pole, you know."

"I'm sure you'll think of something, dear," said Sophie. "Come, little Santa, let's start packing."

F O U R

AND SO THE CLAUS FAMILY moved to the North Pole.

At first it was tough sledding for them all. Everywhere they looked was snow and ice. There were no trees, no flowers, no grass, and no shopping malls. There were only glaciers.

It was cold.

It was so cold that whenever they exhaled, their breath froze and caused a mini-hailstorm at their feet.

It was so cold that their words froze right in the air, and if you couldn't hear them, you could read them.

It was so cold that if they didn't walk fast enough, their feet froze right to the ground. Whenever that

ABERNETHY

happened, Milton used a portable propane blowtorch to melt them free.

The Claus family rented a two-bedroom house in a neighborhood of Eskimos. They soon began to learn the ways of the Eskimos.

They ate fish every day for dinner. And every day for lunch. And every day for breakfast. The fish wasn't even cooked. Most of the time the fish wasn't even thawed. After a while, they grew so accustomed to frozen food, they ate TV dinners without bothering to thaw them out.

There were other things besides the cold the Claus family had to get used to at the North Pole. Polar bears. Penguins. Walruses. Seals. Whale blubber. Huskies. Packs of hungry wolves. The Northern Lights. And the fact that the days and nights there were six months long.

In fact, days and nights that were six months long were even harder to get used to than unthawed TV dinners. Same-day service at the cleaners sometimes took half a year.

Milton Claus did indeed find a sleigh to haul around the iceboxes he sold door to door, but the eight tiny walruses he found to pull it were painfully slow.

 F  I  V  E

FOR CHRISTMAS THAT FIRST year at the North Pole, Sophie and Milton bought little Santa a pair of red ice skates, a red sled, a shiny red fire truck, and a little red wagon. Milton bought Sophie a red flannel nightgown. Sophie bought Milton a suit of long red underwear.

Milton was sad. He missed Sioux City and the somewhat milder winters. Little Santa bought his father a joke book to cheer him up.

Milton read several jokes from the book out loud at the dinner table.

"A pygmy walks into a Miami Beach hotel," is the way one of them began.

"So I happen to like bananas," is the way one of them ended.

Sophie chuckled politely, but little Santa roared "Ho, ho, ho!" after every joke.

"Our son appears to have quite a sense of humor," said Milton.

The next day at nursery school, little Santa asked his classmates what presents they received on Christmas. Some of the children came from very poor families. Unlike the Clauses, these parents couldn't afford to buy toys, so for Christmas, they'd given their children dead fish. Little Santa was so upset to hear this he insisted upon giving the children his own toys.

"Our son has quite a generous nature," said Milton.

"He certainly does," said Sophie.

"A little *too* generous, if you ask me," said Milton.

WHEN YOUNG SANTA WAS six, he announced to his parents that he had decided what he wanted to be when he grew up.

"What?" said both Sophie and Milton together.

"A fireman," said young Santa proudly.

"And why would you like to be a fireman?" asked Milton. "To put out fires?"

"Well, yeah," said young Santa, "but that's not the main reason."

"To save people?" said Sophie.

"Well, yeah, that, too," said young Santa, "but that's not the main reason."

"Then why?" asked Milton.

"Because red is such a beautiful color," said young Santa. "I'd rather wear it than any other color."

"But firemen don't *wear* red," said Sophie.

"They don't?" said young Santa.

"No," said Sophie.

"Oh," said young Santa.

Shortly after that, young Santa decided that a fireman wasn't what he wanted to be when he grew up, after all. To cheer him up, Sophie sewed him a beautiful red suit trimmed in white fur. He loved it so much that from the moment he put it on, he would wear nothing else. On warm days, he sweated a lot.

By the time young Santa turned eight, he was so good at his studies that he usually finished his homework every night about ten minutes after he got home. He seemed bored.

"When are they going to invent television?" he asked his mother.

"I'm sure I don't know," replied Sophie. "Why don't you find a nice after-school activity, dear?"

"Like what?" said young Santa.

"Like how's about joining the Cub Scouts?" said Sophie.

"The Cub Scouts. That sounds like just the thing for me," said young Santa.

But shortly after joining the Cub Scouts, he learned that all the other members of his den were polar bear cubs and not boys, and eventually he quit.

When he was ten, young Santa's favorite subject was geography. He loved hearing about each country's customs. He seemed particularly interested in hearing how each country celebrated Christmas.

He was also fascinated with maps. He kept asking his teachers how long it might take to go from one country

to another. After a while, they began to kid him.

"What are you planning to do, young Santa," asked one teacher, smiling, "visit a whole bunch of countries in a single night?"

"Oh, if only that were possible," young Santa would dreamily reply.

"Well, maybe by the time you grow up," said his teachers, "they'll have invented jet planes. Then you can visit a whole bunch of countries in a single night."

"Do you really think that might happen someday?" asked young Santa excitedly.

"Personally, I doubt it," said his teacher. "But then, I never thought you'd find a way to open cans electrically, either. Tell me, what would you do if you could visit a whole bunch of countries in a single night?"

"Gosh, I don't know," said young Santa. "Deliver pizza maybe?"

 S  E  V  E  N

ONE MORNING SHORTLY after his thirteenth birthday, young Santa woke up and felt something funny on his cheeks. He went into the bathroom and took a look in the medicine-cabinet mirror.

"Oh my gosh," said young Santa, "I've begun to grow hair on my cheeks!"

Milton walked into the bathroom and gazed at his son proudly.

"Congratulations, son," he said, "your beard has begun to grow. Let me give you your first lesson in shaving."

And so Milton showed young Santa how to apply the shaving cream with a fluffy brush, and then to shave it off with the sure, clean strokes of a well-stropped razor.

"There, now," said Milton, "look at your cheeks, son. What do you see there instead of short stubby hairs?"

"A rash," said young Santa.

"What?" said Milton.

Milton leaned in close and studied young Santa's cheeks. Sure enough, young Santa had developed a shaving rash.

"Must be you're allergic to this brand of shaving lotion," said Milton. "So tomorrow we'll try another."

But switching brands of shaving lotion didn't help. Neither did switching brands of razors.

"Why can't I just let my beard grow?" asked young Santa.

"Why?" said Milton. "I'll tell you why. Because if you just let your beard grow when you're a teenager, then by

the time you're an old man, you'll have a long white beard, that's why."

"And what would be so bad about that?" asked young Santa.

Milton thought about it and couldn't come up with an answer, so young Santa simply stopped shaving.

E I G H T

WHEN YOUNG SANTA WAS fourteen, he applied for and received his learner's permit. Milton began to teach him how to drive the family sleigh. At first, getting the eight tiny walruses to start and stop and turn smoothly was hard for the boy, but eventually he began to get a real feel for it.

Soon he was driving the sleigh so skillfully that his dad often took him along when he called on people to sell them iceboxes. Milton felt confident enough to give young Santa the reins for long stretches of roadway. He took them back from him only when they neared areas where they might pass traffic policemen—traffic policemen who wouldn't know what an excellent sleigh driver young Santa had become and would see only a boy with a beard driving a sleigh without a license.

On young Santa's sixteenth birthday, he earned his

official driver's license. The inspector from the driver's license bureau who tested young Santa couldn't believe how well the young man had done.

"We don't often give compliments in my line of work, young fella," he said, "but I have to tell you—as a sleigh driver, you're some kind of all right."

"Thank you, sir," said young Santa, as proud as he could be.

To show their confidence in him, Sophie and Milton allowed him to take the sleigh out by himself on short excursions.

Young Santa drove the sleigh by the high school and all his classmates gathered around to look at it. Most of

them admired it. But some of them were jealous and made fun of the rickety sleigh and of the eight tiny walruses who pulled it.

"Hey, how long does it take that thing to go from zero to sixty," asked one, "half an hour?"

"Yeah, half an hour," said another, "and that's when it's hitting on all sixteen flippers!"

"Oh, you're hurting the walruses' feelings—tusk, tusk!" quipped a third.

Young Santa chuckled politely, but his friends' jokes stung. When he got home, Sophie and Milton asked him how his friends had liked the sleigh.

"Oh, okay, I guess," said young Santa. "But you know, these walruses are really slow, Milt. Couldn't we trade them in for something with a little more zip?"

"Milt?" said Milton, with a frown.

"Don't be disrespectful, young Santa," said Sophie. "Your father's name is either Dad or Milton. It is most certainly not Milt."

"Sorry," sighed young Santa. "These walruses are so slow, *Dad*, don't you think we could trade them in for something with a little more zip?"

"Like what," said his father, "penguins?"

"Like, I don't know, like maybe eight tiny reindeer," said young Santa.

"Reindeer?" scoffed his father. "Our sleigh could never handle all that power."

"Aww, Dad," said young Santa.

"Besides," said Milton Claus, "how do you suggest we pay for them? I certainly can't afford eight tiny reindeer on an icebox salesman's salary."

"Maybe I could get a job after school," said young Santa.

Milton Claus saw how much young Santa wanted a more powerful sleigh. He loved his son very much and hated to deprive him of anything.

"Tell you what, son," he said. "Why don't we just

mosey on downtown to the sleigh showrooms and look over this year's models?"

Young Santa let out a whoop of joy.

"Now I'm not saying we can afford to buy anything," said his father. "But last I heard, just *looking* didn't cost anything."

THAT YEAR'S MODELS OF reindeer sleighs were very exciting. They came in V-6's and V-8's. Needless to say, the teams of eight were much more powerful than the teams of six. The reindeer were thoroughbreds from Iceland and Lapland and looked big and powerful. Their harnesses were made of shiny red leather trimmed in silver or gold.

The sleighs themselves were sleek and low to the ground and looked as though they would go like the wind. They had beautiful red leather tuck-and-roll seats. There was an extra-powerful model made by Ferrari, a fiberglass model made by Corvette, and even one by DeLorean with gull-wing doors.

They were all so expensive that young Santa knew it was hopeless to even dream of owning one.

"What do you think, son?" said Milton, with a sad smile on his face.

"Well, they're nice, Dad," said young Santa, "but I don't really like them as much as I thought I would."

"You don't?" said Milton.

"Nah," said young Santa. "I think they're too souped up. I don't think you could drive them anywhere but Indianapolis or LeMans."

Milton knew what his son was doing and appreciated his thoughtfulness.

"Why don't we go to a used-sleigh lot and see what they've got in stock," said Milton.

T E N

THE USED-SLEIGH LOT WAS not as fancy as the new sleigh showrooms, but the stock was better than either young Santa or his father expected.

True, some of the sleighs had dents in their sides and rusted runners, and some of the reindeer had prongs broken off their antlers, but what they lacked in shine, they more than made up for in spunk.

"Well, well, gents," said a fellow in a houndstooth-checked parka and a loud tie, walking up to them, rubbing his hands. "And what can I do you for today?"

Young Santa looked at the used-sleigh salesman a bit dubiously and turned to his father.

"We were just browsing, really," said Milton Claus.

"Browse all you like," said the used-sleigh salesman. "And when you're ready to talk turkey, you just let me know."

"Why would we want to talk about turkeys?"

whispered young Santa to his dad. "Turkeys aren't strong enough to pull sleighs, are they?"

"Talking turkey is a figure of speech, son," said his father. "It means speaking about how much money we might be willing to pay."

"You mean we might be able to afford one of those sleighs they have for sale here?" said young Santa delightedly.

"Could be," said his dad with a twinkle, "could be."

They looked carefully at all the sleighs on display in the lot.

"Kick the runners if you like," said the salesman.

"Why would we want to kick the runners?" asked young Santa.

"To see how sturdy they are," said the salesman.

One sleigh in particular caught young Santa's fancy. It was big and roomy and he thought his dad would like it because it could hold a lot of iceboxes. But the lines were kind of sporty, and the seats were wide and comfortable, so he thought he'd enjoy driving it himself.

The salesman saw young Santa admiring the sleigh.

"Like that one, kid?" he said. "That one's a doozy. Happens to have very low mileage, too, on account of it was owned by a little old lady in Pascagoula who only used it after heavy blizzards."

"Pascagoula?" said young Santa. "Isn't that in Mississippi on the Gulf of Mexico?"

"Kid knows his geography, I see," said the salesman, winking at Milton Claus.

"I don't think it snows at *all* in Mississippi," said young Santa.

"That's what I'm saying," said the salesman. "Now then, if that's the sleigh you like best, the next step is to fix you up with the right power package. You see any reindeer that particularly catch your eye?"

"Gosh," said young Santa, looking nervously at his dad, "we were only browsing. . . ."

"That's okay, son," said Milton. "If you like that sleigh, I think we can afford it. Depending on what kind of team you pick to go with it."

Young Santa flashed his father a grateful smile.

"A sled that big, of course," said the salesman, "you're looking at a team of eight."

"Gosh, son," said Milton apologetically, "I'm afraid we can't afford an eight. On an icebox salesman's salary, the most I can afford is a six."

"A six, eh?" said the salesman, frowning. "That's a shame, sir. This particular sled here is just too heavy for a six."

Young Santa's face fell. But then the salesman had an idea.

"Tell you what," he said. "I just got a team I can let you have a price on."

"A six?" said young Santa.

The salesman shook his head.

"No, no, it's an eight," he said, "but I can let you have them for the price of a six."

"Why?" said Milton. "What's wrong with them?"

"Nothing," said the salesman. "They're a little undersized is all."

And with that, he led the way over to a barn at the edge of the lot and motioned for young Santa and his dad to look inside. They did, and gasped.

Inside the barn, calmly munching hay, were eight tiny reindeer. They were perfect.

"They're small, but they're pretty feisty little guys," said the salesman. "They oughta be able to pull the sled you got your eye on. I'll give you the eight for the price of a six. What do you say?"

Young Santa looked questioningly at his dad. His dad smiled.

"I say you've got yourself a deal," said Milton Claus.

Young Santa hugged his dad. His dad shook hands

with the salesman. And then young Santa went to pet the eight tiny reindeer.

"What are their names?" said young Santa.

"Uh, let me see," said the salesman. "Well, there's Dasher and Dancer and Prancer and Vixen. There's Comet and Cupid and Donder and Blitzen . . ."

"Donder and Blitzen?" said Milton.

"I took 'em on a trade for a Volkswagen from some old German guy," said the salesman. "You can change their names to anything you want."

E L E V E N

To HELP PAY FOR THE NEW sleigh and reindeer, the very next day, young Santa went to work in the toy department of the North Pole's only department store.

The store manager took an immediate shine to the boy. After young Santa's second day of work, the manager, who was always looking for ways to drum up business, took the boy aside.

"Listen, kid," he said, "Christmas is in three weeks. If we had some kind of promotional gimmick, I think we could pull a lot of people into the store."

"Like what?" said young Santa.

"Like maybe having you sit down on a big chair," said the manager, "and asking all the little kids to climb up in your lap and tell you what they had for breakfast."

Young Santa frowned. He didn't think this was much of an idea, but he liked the manager and he didn't want to hurt his feelings.

"If you really think that'll pull people into the store," young Santa said, "then let's take a shot at it."

So the store manager put up signs all over the store.

TELL SANTA WHAT YOU HAD FOR BREAKFAST! they proclaimed in huge letters. WHAT DID YOU EAT THIS MORNING? SANTA WANTS TO KNOW!

Only one kid showed up, an Eskimo boy.

"Ho, ho, ho," said young Santa, as the little boy climbed up into his lap, "and what did you have for breakfast today, young man?"

The boy looked at Santa suspiciously.

"What do you care what I had for breakfast?" he said.

"Well," said young Santa, who didn't care and was just asking in order to humor the store manager, "Santa likes to know these things."

"Okay," said the boy, "I had Pop-Tarts."

"Ah," said young Santa, not knowing what else to say. "What flavor Pop-Tarts?"

"Fish," said the boy.

"*Fish*-flavor Pop-Tarts?" said young Santa.

"Yeah," said the boy.

"Yum," said young Santa, not wishing to hurt the boy's feelings.

Nobody else came by to tell young Santa what they had for breakfast.

The store manager was depressed.

"Let's face it," said the store manager, "my idea was a dud. A clunker. A total washout. I'm sorry I ever thought of it."

"It was a nice idea, sir," said young Santa. "But it just didn't pull people into the store."

"I know," said the manager sadly.

But then his face brightened.

"Hey," he said, "what about if they climbed up in your lap and told you what they dreamed about the night before?"

"Since our nights are six months long," said young Santa, "that might take too much time."

"Mmmm, you have a point there," said the manager.

Both he and young Santa were silent a long time, each trying to come up with a better idea.

"Hey," said young Santa after a while, "what about

this? What if kids climbed up in my lap and told me what they wanted for Christmas?"

The manager thought this over. Then he shook his head.

"Nah," he said. "Who's going to care about telling you what they want for Christmas?"

"I guess you're probably right," said young Santa. "Still, why not give it a try, anyway?"

"Well," said the manager, "I suppose we could do that. I mean what else have we got going for us, right?"

"Right," said young Santa.

"Okay," said the manager, "let's give it a shot."

And so that very afternoon, young Santa got up on a big chair in the toy department and encouraged the small children who were there to come up and sit in his lap and tell him what they wanted for Christmas.

The kids liked talking about what they wanted for Christmas more than talking about what they'd had for breakfast, and they liked talking to young Santa. They told their friends and the idea caught on.

Soon the lines of kids waiting to tell young Santa what they wanted for Christmas stretched clear around the block. And the store sold toys faster than they could get them from the factory.

YOUNG SANTA WAS PROUD of how many toys were being sold because of his success in talking to kids about what they wanted for Christmas. He expected this success would make the store manager happy. But he was wrong.

Young Santa found the manager in the stockroom of the store, worriedly watching huge cartons of toys being unpacked and rushed out to the waiting customers.

"This keeps up," said the manager, stroking his chin, "we're going to run clear out of toys. Then what?"

"Then maybe we'll have to do something else to get them," said young Santa.

"Like what?" said the manager.

"Like what?" said young Santa. "Like, I don't know, like maybe making our own."

"You're kidding me," said the manager.

"No," said young Santa, "actually I was serious."

"What, you mean you and *me* should make the toys?" said the manager.

"Why not?" said young Santa.

"How about I don't know how?" said the manager. "How about I could cut my finger? Plus which, if I sat around making toys all day, who would run the store, would you tell me that? Uh-uh. Thanks, but no thanks, kid, I'm not sitting around making any toys."

"Well, then, maybe you could hire somebody to make the toys for you," said young Santa.

"Yeah?" said the manager. "Who you got in mind?"

"I don't know," said young Santa. "How about out-of-work Eskimos?"

"Have you ever seen any out-of-work Eskimos?" said the manager.

"Well, no, now that you mention it, I haven't," said young Santa.

"There aren't any out-of-work Eskimos is the reason," said the manager.

"Well, then, how about somebody else?" said young Santa. "How about elves?"

"Elves!" The manager laughed.

"What's wrong with elves?" said young Santa.

"All elves know how to do is make shoes," said the manager.

"They could be retrained to make toys," said young Santa. "And the beauty of it is that there are so many of them without jobs."

"You know, kid," said the manager, "you may just have a point there."

And so it was that the elves were hired to make the toys.

At first the elves seemed confused. All the toys they made came out looking like shoes. There were shoe-like dolls and shoe-like teddy bears and shoe-like cars and shoe-like trucks and shoe-like locomotives and shoe-like hobbyhorses.

Young Santa pointed out to the elves where they were going wrong, and soon they began to get the hang of it. The dolls began looking more like dolls, the teddy bears more like teddy bears, the cars more like cars, the trucks more like trucks, and the locomotives more like locomotives.

Only the rocking horses still looked a little like bedroom slippers.

A WEEK BEFORE CHRISTMAS, a huge blizzard came up. The wind blew so furiously and the snow flew so fast that the store's trucks could not deliver any of the elf-made toys to all the good girls and boys on Christmas Eve.

The manager was at his wits' end.

"What the heck am I going to do with all these toys?" he said. "Eat them?"

"Of course not," said young Santa. "What would be the point of eating them?"

"It was just a figure of speech, kid," said the manager. "But how are we going to deliver them? Our trucks can't get any traction on the glacier, especially during a blizzard."

"If only we had something like a . . . a sleigh or something," said one of the elves.

"A sleigh?" said young Santa. "Why, my dad has a sleigh."

"Really?" said another elf. "Do you think he'd lend it to us?"

"Gosh, I don't think so," said young Santa. "He needs that sleigh every day for his work."

"What about after work on the night before Christmas?" asked another elf. "Do you think he'd lend it to us then?"

"I don't know," said young Santa. "He's a little leery about lending it to strangers."

"Then maybe we could hire him to drive it himself," said the manager.

"Boy, I doubt it," said young Santa. "When my dad gets home from work every night, he's so bushed he can barely see straight."

The manager and the elves were quite depressed. Unless they thought of something soon, the good girls and boys would never get their toys in time for Christmas.

"Listen" said young Santa, "this is probably a long shot, but I could ask Dad to lend *me* the sleigh on Christmas Eve."

"You think he'd go for it?" said an elf.

"Not if I tell him I'm going to try and deliver all those toys myself," said young Santa. "But if I let him think I'm just going out for a little fun, he might let me do it."

"If only you could do that," said the manager, "we'd be saved."

"I'll try my best," said young Santa.

"We're counting on you, kid," said an elf.

On Christmas Eve after dinner, young Santa cleared away the dishes and stacked them in the dishwasher and then asked his father if he could borrow the sleigh.

"Gosh, I don't know, son," said Milton Claus. "You've only just gotten your driver's license."

"But I'm good, Dad," said young Santa, "you told me so yourself."

"Yes," said his father, "but you're still a little rusty on your left turns, and you hardly know how to parallel park at all."

"Aww, c'mon, Dad," said young Santa. "I'll really be careful. And besides, I kind of promised the guys."

"Driving in this blizzard is too dangerous," said Milton.

"No, look," said young Santa, going to the window and pushing back the curtains, "it's letting up. In fact, it's almost stopped."

Young Santa's father peered outside at the deep drifts of snow. The blizzard had, indeed, almost stopped. The clouds were drifting away, and in the distant sky, he could see the multicolored Northern Lights.

"Oh, let him take the sleigh, Milton," said Sophie Claus. "He's been working so hard after school at the store, he deserves a little fun."

"Well . . . all right," sighed young Santa's dad, "if you promise to drive extra carefully and have the sleigh home early."

"Oh, I promise, Dad," said young Santa happily. "And the guys will really be delighted."

"I'll bet they will," said Milton.

Young Santa put on his red snowsuit and cap with the white fur trim. He was excited at the opportunity of delivering toys to all the good girls and boys. He wondered how he would carry the toys from the sleigh to the children's houses.

"Mom, do you have a big old laundry bag I could borrow?" said young Santa.

"What on earth would you want with a big old laundry bag?" said Sophie.

"I'll tell you tomorrow," said young Santa with a mischievous wink.

"Oh, you're such a tease," said his mother and gave him the laundry bag.

Young Santa threw the empty bag over his shoulder, then kissed his mom and dad good night.

"That sleigh really moves with those eight tiny reindeer," said Milton, "so for heaven's sake, don't speed."

"I won't," said young Santa. "I promise."

"You get a speeding ticket, young man," said Milton, "and you're grounded for a year."

"I promise you I won't get a ticket," said young Santa. " 'Bye, Mom. 'Bye, Dad. Merry Christmas! Ho, ho, ho!"

"Well, you're certainly in a good mood," said Sophie.

"Say hello to the guys," said Milton.

"I will," said young Santa and left.

"What guys?" said Sophie.

"I don't know," said Milton. "Didn't he say 'I promised the guys?' "

FIFTEEN

YOUNG SANTA GOT INTO HIS father's sleigh and clucked to the reindeer. The reindeer lurched forward with such force that he was thrown against the back of the seat. The trip to the department store in the empty sleigh took less than five minutes.

When the manager and the elves saw young Santa's sleigh shudder and skid to a stop at the loading entrance to the store in a shower of snow, they burst into cheers.

"Hooray for young Santa! Way to go, kid! Good going, babe!" cried the elves.

The manager told them to stop cheering and start loading presents. It was already getting late and young Santa had too many houses on his delivery route as it was.

The elves scurried back and forth between sleigh and workshop, their little elf arms clasping wrapped toys, until the sleigh was piled with so many presents it sank deep into the loosely packed snow.

Young Santa climbed up into the driver's seat of the sleigh and waved good-bye.

"Drive safely, kid!" said the manager.

"You pull this off, you're a real hero," said one elf.

"And if you don't, you're a bum," said another elf.

"Merry Christmas to all," said young Santa, "and to all, uh . . . have a nice day!"

He put the sleigh in gear and clucked to the reindeer, but nothing happened. The sleigh was so heavy with presents it wouldn't move.

He looked at the instruction manual in the glove compartment, then said slowly and carefully out loud: "Now, Dasher! Now, Dancer! Now, Prancer and Vixen! On Comet! On, Cupid! On, Donder and Blitzen!"

The heavy sleigh lurched forward. It was loaded with gifts, but the eight turbocharged reindeer pulled so hard it began plowing through the snow. Two plumes of snow, one on each side, arose in its wake.

But young Santa, who was not even comfortable driving the sleigh empty, now found the added weight made the sleigh too hard to steer. He tried his best to control it, but the heavy sleigh skidded and swayed dangerously from side to side.

Making a sharp right turn in the center of town, the sleigh went into a skid, sideswiped a dogsled and a team of huskies, narrowly missed a polar bear who had moseyed into town looking for something to eat, and went

careening into a snowbank. Half the presents the elves had loaded toppled off the sleigh and into the snow.

"Oh, no," said young Santa.

He got out and went over to the reindeer.

"Anybody hurt?" he asked.

The reindeer shook their heads.

The sound of a police siren sent a shudder through him.

"Oh, no," said young Santa.

The police car skidded to a stop beside the sleigh, its dome lights flashing. Two policemen hopped out of the car and scurried over to the sleigh.

"Anybody hurt?" said the first policeman.

"No, sir," said young Santa.

"Can I see your license and registration, young fella?" said the second policeman.

Young Santa fished in the side pocket of his red suit with the white fur trim. He was extremely nervous. Had he left home without his license? That would be terrible. No, thank heavens, there it was!

"Here, officers," said Santa. "Are you g-going to give me a ticket?"

"Do you know how fast you were going?" said the first policeman.

"N-no, I don't," said young Santa.

"Neither do we," said the first policeman, "but it must have been well over the limit."

"Yeah," said the second policeman, "you were really flying."

"I guess I was going pretty fast," said young Santa truthfully.

"I don't mean you were going fast, kid," said the policeman, "I mean you were *flying*. A foot off the ground at times. Did you know that?"

"I sure didn't," said young Santa. He was embarrassed to find out he'd been flying, but he was also a little excited and proud. "I guess I was hitting on all eight. These reindeer must have even more power than I thought."

The policeman shone a flashlight on young Santa's driver's license.

"Santa . . . Claus," he read aloud. "That you, kid?"

"Yes, sir," said young Santa.

"What kind of a name is Santa?" said the policeman.

"My mom said it was in memory of a nice vacation my folks had had just before I was born," replied young Santa.

"They went to Santa Barbara?" asked the policeman.

"No, Santa Fe," said young Santa.

"Santa Fe, eh?" said the policeman. "This registration here is made out to one Milton Claus. That your pop?"

"Yes, sir," said young Santa.

"He know you're out, tearing around town in a sleigh piled high with presents?" asked the policeman.

"Well, uh, yes and no," said young Santa.

" 'Yes and no'?" said the policeman suspiciously. "What does that mean?"

"I mean he knows I'm out—he gave me the sleigh for the evening," said young Santa. "But, uh, he may not know about the presents."

"Why?" said the policeman. "They hot?"

"Oh, no, sir, they're not hot," said young Santa, "I'm sure they're as cold as I am."

"Don't be a wise guy," said the policeman. "I meant are they stolen?"

"*Stolen!*" said young Santa. "Gosh, no. I'm delivering them for the department store."

"We can check on that, you know," said the other policeman. "Who you delivering them to at this time of night, fella?"

"Good girls and boys," said young Santa.

"Good girls and boys, eh?" said the first policeman. "And what are you bringing them, if I may ask?"

"Toys," said young Santa. "Toys made by elves."

"Toys made by elves, eh?" said the second policeman. "All right, kid, I think you'd better come back to the station house with us."

"Oh, no, please, officer," said young Santa in a panic. "If you give me a ticket, then my dad will ground me for a year. And what's even worse, if I come back to the station house with you, the good girls and boys will never get their presents in time for Christmas!"

The two policemen looked at young Santa and then at each other. Then they looked at young Santa. Then they looked at each other. Then they looked back at young Santa.

"What we ought to do," said the first policeman, "we ought to run you into the station house and give you a citation for speeding, reckless driving, and flying without a pilot's license. That's what we ought to do. . . ."

"But being as how it's Christmas Eve and all," said the second policeman, "we're just going to let you off with a warning."

"Oh, thank you, officers," said young Santa gratefully.

"You better drive carefully, though, kid," said the first policeman. "We catch you speeding or flying again, we'll write you up for sure."

"I understand, officers," said young Santa, "and thank you."

"Merry Christmas, son," said the first policeman, climbing back into the patrol car.

"Yeah, Merry Christmas," said the second, climbing in after him.

"Merry Christmas to all," said young Santa, "and to all a, uh . . . very pleasant Yuletide season."

SIXTEEN

YOUNG SANTA BREATHED A huge sigh of relief, then picked up all the presents that had fallen off into the snow and piled them back on the sleigh.

It had been late when he left home for the department store, later yet by the time the elves had loaded the sleigh and he'd gotten under way. Because of the accident and being stopped by the police, he was now so late that everyone he was delivering presents to had surely gone to bed. How could he deliver presents to them if they were asleep?

Young Santa got back into the driver's seat and put

the sleigh in reverse. The heavy sleigh moved back slowly. Clear of the snowbank, young Santa put it in forward gear.

"Now, Dasher," he said cautiously, "now, Dancer . . . please be careful, guys, so this kind of thing doesn't happen again, okay?"

The reindeer bobbed their heads as though they understood, and the sleigh moved forward.

At first the reindeer went slowly and carefully. But soon, the sheer pleasure of dashing through the snow, pulling a sleigh full of toys for good girls and boys on Christmas Eve, made them giddy with joy. And before young Santa could say "Whoa!" they were once more whizzing through the snow. And before he knew it, the first house on his delivery schedule came into view.

"There it is!" cried young Santa excitedly. "Our first stop! Whoa! Whoa!"

Once more, young Santa badly misjudged the weight and speed of the sleigh. When he pulled back on the reins, it didn't slow the sleigh, it only forced the back end down. With the back end down, the front end went up, and the eight tiny reindeer pulled straight into the air in a takeoff as steep as that of a 747.

To the top of the porch, to the top of the wall, and up to the housetop they flew. The sleigh skidded crazily across the snow-covered roof and slammed into the chimney.

"Whew!" said young Santa, a little shaken up by the dramatic stop. "You guys okay?"

The reindeer bobbed their heads, assuring him they were.

Young Santa stepped gingerly out of the sleigh and onto the roof. From within the house, he heard people stirring. Then somebody flew to the window, tore open the shutters, and threw up the sash. A man stuck his head out and looked around.

"Who's out there?" yelled the man.

Young Santa said nothing.

"We've just settled our brains for a long winter's nap here," said the man. "You want to give us a break or what?"

Young Santa held his breath, terrified of revealing his presence. If the store ever found out this was the way he was delivering gifts to the good girls and boys, he'd be fired for sure! He motioned to the reindeer to remain silent.

After a few moments, the man swore softly, pulled his head back inside, shut the window, and went to bed.

Now young Santa had a problem. He was supposed to deliver toys to the good girls and boys inside the house, but he was too scared to go to the front door, ring the bell, and get the man out of bed again.

He didn't know what to do.

He carefully put the children's presents into his mom's laundry bag and picked his way across the roof. Perhaps if he could find an open window, he could just quietly reach his arm in and drop the gifts inside, one by one.

He crawled to the edge of the slanted, snow-covered roof and hung upside down over the edge, peering into the topmost windows.

They were all closed and locked. He pulled himself back up to the roof.

Between him and the windows on the other side of the house was a fat brick chimney. With the sleigh and the eight reindeer parked there, young Santa didn't have enough room to step around it. To reach the other windows, he'd have to climb over the chimney.

He slung his bag of toys over his shoulder and very carefully shinnied his way to the top of the chimney. Standing on the very edge of it, he tried to get his balance.

A sudden gust of wind blew him backward. He lost his balance and before he knew it he was plunging right down the chimney, bag and all!

With a tremendous clatter, he landed in the hearth on a pile of smoldering logs.

"Ouch!" said young Santa, leaping to his feet and rubbing the smoking seat of his trousers.

"Hey!" yelled the voice of the man who had appeared at the window. "Is there somebody downstairs?"

"Oh-oh," said young Santa softly, "I'd better leave those gifts and get out of here fast!"

"Dear, I think there are robbers in the living room," said a woman's voice. "You'd better call the police!"

"I'll do better than that," said the man's voice. "I'll get my shotgun!"

As fast as he could, young Santa took the presents for the good girls and boys out of his mother's laundry bag and looked about for a suitable place to leave them. He dared not stray far from the shelter of the fireplace.

In the gloom of the darkened living room, he saw a clothesline which had been stretched across the front of the hearth. On the clothesline was wet laundry which had been hung up to dry near the warmth of the fire: undershorts, stockings, and panty hose.

Young Santa jammed toys into the undershorts, stockings, and panty hose, just as the light in the hallway outside the living room snapped on. He heard heavy feet rapidly coming down the stairs.

Young Santa tied his empty bag around his waist and tried to shinny back up the inside of the chimney. He couldn't get a foothold. He kept sliding. Sliding down the chimney was a better way to get into a house than it was to get out of one.

Young Santa wedged himself into the chimney and began climbing upward as quietly as he could. When his feet had cleared the top edge of the fireplace, the light in the living room came on.

Young Santa held his breath.

"Who's there?" yelled the man.

Young Santa said nothing. To come out of the chimney now, covered with soot and ashes and holding an empty sack, would probably not be the wisest move in the world.

"I know you're there somewhere," said the man, "and I've got a gun."

Young Santa continued to say nothing.

"Is it robbers, dear?" said the woman's voice.

"I don't know," said the man. "I don't see anyone. Maybe it was just . . . well, I'll be hornswoggled!"

"What is it, dear?" said the woman.

Young Santa, to his terror, heard the man's footsteps approach the fireplace. His heart began beating so loudly in his chest he was sure the man could hear him.

"What is it, dear?" called the woman nervously.

"Some idiot has broken into our house and stuffed presents in our underwear!" said the man.

"What?" called the woman.

"I said some moron snuck in here and jammed gifts in our skivvies!" said the man.

"Someone broke into our house?" shrieked the woman. "Oh, no! Oh, help!"

"Calm down!" yelled the man. "They didn't take anything, they *gave* us something!"

"What?" yelled the woman, "they did *what?*"

"Just calm down for a second and I'll show you!" yelled the man.

Young Santa heard the man stack his shotgun against the wall, disconnect the clothesline, and walk back toward the hall.

"Look," called the man, "presents! Presents from robbers! Are you ready for this?"

As soon as the man left the living room, young Santa shinnied the rest of the way up the chimney and crawled out onto the roof. His face and hands and his beautiful red suit were black. He slapped himself free of soot and ashes and took a deep breath of fresh, cold North Pole air.

Young Santa felt lucky to be alive. What a close call he'd had!

He climbed back into the driver's seat, called softly to his reindeer, and, to his surprise, the sleigh rose once more into the air. His heart was still pounding, but his eyes were twinkling.

The experience of delivering toys to the first house had been frightening. It had also been the most exciting, the most satisfying and exhilarating thing he had ever done in his life. He knew that delivering the rest of the presents would be easier and just as much fun.

Young Santa was still too young to have chosen a career, but if he could ever find something as much fun as delivering presents on Christmas Eve, he knew he'd be a truly happy man!

## ABOUT THE AUTHOR AND ILLUSTRATOR

DAN GREENBURG says, "One day I got to wondering about Santa Claus and how he got to be who he is today. I mean, he wasn't born a fat old guy with a white beard, right? So what was he like as a baby? As a toddler? And, most important of all, what was Santa like as a teenager? To answer these perplexing questions, I wrote this book."

Dan Greenburg is the author of several best-selling adult books, including *How to be a Jewish Mother, How to Avoid Love and Marriage, Confessions of a Pregnant Father,* and the children's books, *Jumbo the Boy and Arnold the Elephant* and *The Bed Who Ran Away from Home.* Born in Chicago, Mr. Greenburg is a relatively new father who now lives in New York.

WARREN MILLER has been a staff cartoonist with *The New Yorker* magazine since 1961. His work has been published in two collections, and can be found in group collections from *The New Yorker, Playboy,* the Cartoonists Guild, and other magazines. His cartoons have been in exhibitions in the U.S., Canada, and England. Mr. Miller also paints in oils or any other stuff that's handy, and has been known to play jazz on a flügelhorn on rare occasions.

Born in Chicago, Warren Miller lives in New York City with his wife, who teaches biochemistry, and his younger daughter who, at the age of nine, loves to sing like Ethel Merman. His older daughter works 9 to 5 and does stand-up comedy in the evenings. His son lives in California and is an aspiring historian/journalist.

GRE         Greenburg, Dan
            Young Santa

$13.95

| DATE | | | |
|---|---|---|---|
| | | | |
| | | | |
| | | | |
| | | | |
| | | | |
| | | | |
| | | | |
| | | | |
| | | | |
| | | | |
| | | | |
| | | | |